CHATTERBOX BEAR

PIPPA CURNICK

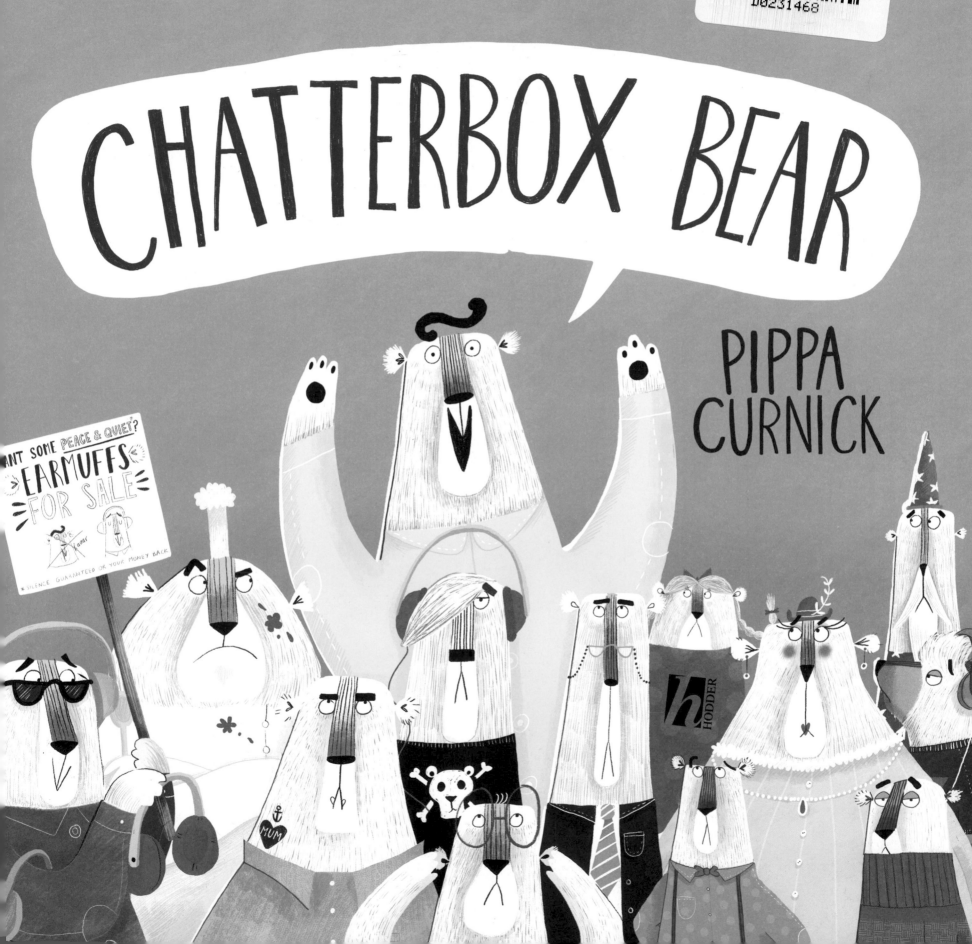

Gary was the world's BIGGEST CHATTERBOX!

Raaar!

He chatted everywhere, to everyone, all the time...

Raaar! Raaar!

in the bath,

in the supermarket,

and EVEN in the library!

The other bears just wanted some peace and quiet.

It made Gary very sad.
"SOMEBODY, SOMEWHERE
must like chatting
as much as I do!"

Raaar.

So Gary packed his bag,
patched up his old boat,

Raaar?

Raaar.

Raaar!

and set out to find
someone to chat to.

At first it was plain sailing . . .

. . . but soon the sea got choppy
and then the boat sprang a leak!

BEAR OVERBOARD!

Luckily, Gary spotted a tiny island . . .

Dot the bird was hopping along the beach when she saw Gary.

"Hello," said Gary raising his amazing, big, black eyebrow.

"Hello," said Dot.
But bears don't speak Bird and all Gary heard was

SQUAWK!

And birds don't speak Bear, so all Dot heard was

Raaar!

Oh dear.

Dot called her friends.
Maybe they could
speak Bear?

SQUAWK

SQUAWK

SQUAWK

SQUAWK

QUAWK

SQUAWK

SQUAWK

But Gary couldn't
understand a word.

Just then, Gary's tummy rumbled.
"I'm so hungry," said Gary,
wobbling his eyebrow.

"Raaar!

Rumble

The birds were baffled.

SQUAWK?
SQUAWK? SQUAWK?

"Does he want to build a nest?" wondered Dot.

"No!" growled Gary.

Gary's eyebrow gave a tremendous wibble-wobble.
"I just want to chat, but no one understands me!"

And he burst into tears.

Dot had been watching Gary very carefully
and she suddenly let out a great

SQUAWK!

"LOOK AT HIS EYEBROW!
It's all droopy and sad.
Maybe he can tell us other
things with his eyebrow?"

Dot handed Gary a stick. He drew
his eyebrow shapes in the sand,
next to a picture of what
each one meant.

hungry

thirsty

very, VERY hot

happy

"I know, let's all learn to speak Bear!" said Dot.
"But first we need eyebrows of our own . . ."

All the birds began copying
Gary's eyebrow movements.

And slowly but surely, they all started to speak the same language!

What a discovery!

"We love our eyebrows," said Dot. "And we LOVE talking Bear."

They celebrated with crab cakes and seaweed doughnuts (Gary's favourite),

and they drank lovely,
bubbly lemonade by moonlight.

It was a perfect
eyebrow party.

The only thing that made it even more perfect was . . .

DANCING!

"COME ON, GARY! Follow our
eyebrows and DANCE!!"
said Dot.

Gary was the happiest he'd ever been.
"I'd like to stay here with you!" he said,
wibbling and wobbling his eyebrow.

"You're all such a lovely bunch
of CHATTERBOXES!"

Just then, the birds spotted something far out at sea. It was getting closer and closer . . .

WANT TO TALK
BEAR?
- - - - - - -
EYEBROWS
FOR
SALE

IT WAS A DOG.
"Hello,"
said Gary.

WOOF?
said Barry, waving his
GIGANTIC MOUSTACHE!

"Oh!" said Dot.
"Can anyone speak Dog?"

WANT TO TALK
BEAR? DOG
MOUSTACHES
EYEBROWS
FOR
SALE

HODDER CHILDREN'S BOOKS

First published in Great Britain in 2019
by Hodder and Stoughton

Text and illustrations © Pippa Curnick 2019

A CIP catalogue record of this book
is available from the British Library.

HB ISBN: 978 1 444 94411 2
PB ISBN: 978 1 444 94412 9

10 9 8 7 6 5 4 3 2 1

Printed and bound in China.

MIX
Paper from
responsible sources
FSC® C104740

Hodder Children's Books
An imprint of
Hachette Children's Group
Part of Hodder and Stoughton
Carmelite House
50 Victoria Embankment
London, EC4Y 0DZ

An Hachette UK Company
www.hachette.co.uk

www.hachettechildrens.co.uk

For Nanny Baddows who told
the best stories with her mouth
Love always, Pippa x